# The Crystal Crown

### By JP Wagner

This is a work of fiction. Similarities to real people, places, or events are entirely coincidental.

THE CRYSTAL CROWN

**First edition. March 1, 2023.**

ISBN: 978-1-990862-09-0

# Also by J P Wagner

**Avantir**

**Talisman Series**

**Standalone**

Watch for more at J P Wagner's site.

For the original Skylark

# Introduction

Thank you for purchasing this book. Please note, this is merely an outline for an eventual full length novel which was originally typed out on a manual typewriter almost 60 years ago. The original manuscript was scanned into electronic format and ran through optical character recognition (OCR) leading to many challenges when editing.

Character note: Lethanerri has gone by many names and if you read more of the stories as they come out, you may find her referred to as Lethanerri, Oruneal (Skylark) or even Starwish.

To speak of Ardan the Grim is to speak of many things. One must tell of how he was the last in a line of men who had stood for far Tharid. A line descended from Ardan the Fair, who left Asbaln that there should be no quarrels with his brother, Randell of Avantir. Both of them being sons of the famous Guardian of the Sword of Avantir, Rorick.

But Ardan was cursed with too much ability. Unlike Ardan the Fair, he was dark, with sea-grey eyes, and a face that seldom showed a smile. So much had he been in the field against the clans of the Nangs that he knew little, save the ways of the warrior. He managed to spend some time at various studies, including the Old Arts of the Letters of the Elder Folk, and he excelled in that as well. In his twentieth year, his father died, and he was chosen to take the place of his father, who was the leader of all the hosts of Tharid. Young indeed, but he had gone into the fields with his father since his fifteenth year, and there was little he did not know about the leading of men and the fighting of battles.

This brought his troubles, for the men of the war-host were determined to make him their king in the place of the new King who had succeeded to the throne. Wyrta the seer spoke to him in these words:

*"In the twentieth year, on spring's first day, seek a path to the West away.*

*Go to the land of the Silver Hair, for thy fate does await thee there."*

The next day was the first day of spring, and Ardan had no notion of leaving so suddenly. But as he went again into the busy streets of Cadair, he was greeted by an old man who said, "May luck follow you on your journey, Lord."

Then melted he into the crowd before the startled Ardan could ask him any questions. Barely had this happened when an old woman, swathed in grey, came to present him with a brooch set with a blue stone, "A gift for one

**11**

going away, and a gift for a maid, whoever she might be."

Ardan was just about to begin his first question when a large barefoot Asbalnian sailor, wine-jar in one hand and a woman in the other, came blustering along. He stopped, straightened, and then said, "Ah, milord, we both be travelling tomorrow, ye and me, but ye be travelling something farther and something longer than I. A drink to travellers, then."

He raised his wine-jar, drank, and was off on his way.

Ardan ceased to question himself then. On the next day he set out and was a long time travelling, for he found himself dodging across the track of a band of migrating Nangs, and was forced many miles to the Northward.

Having reached the edge of Cymruthair, the land of the Elder Folk, the folk of the Silver Hair, he was set afoot when his horse died. He set out walking up through the land, looking here and there at whatever appeared to him. He saw several of the towns of the Elder Folk, but did not go to them. He saw some of the Elder Folk themselves from a distance, but none of them came near to him.

Though he did not know it then, word of his presence has spread throughout the Forbidden Lands, and the Elder Folk had simply decided to leave him alone and see what he would do. So it was that he wandered unhindered within the borders of the Golden Wood, until he came within the borders of the land ruled by Lhoran the Tall, called Errimythn, the Starwood.

Now, it was the custom of Lethanerri, daughter of Lhoran, to walk through the paths of the wood, and as she walked she sang, so fair that she was also named Oruneal, or Skylark. It was at about this time that the Elder Folk lost sight of Ardan for a moment, as they had several times before.

Ardan, by this time, was deep into Errimythn, and he had taken his rest rolled in a blanket beneath a willow. It was early morning when he was wakened by someone singing in the far distance. It was a song of the Cymrutha, and he had done his studies well enough that that he knew most of the words of the song, and those he knew not he could guess. As the singer approached, he saw that it was a young maiden, proud but merry, with silver hair falling round her shoulders.

He sat up and watched her approach, and decided then that he should attempt to make her acquaintance. She had approached to within only a few yards of him before she saw him, so still did he remain. When she saw that he was a Mortal Man, she ceased her song, then turned to flee. Ardan rose, and cried after her in the language of the Elder Folk, "*Feyrannan, lhimfam Oruneal*, wait, fairest Skylark."

Now Lethanerri did not know that Ardan was unaware of her name, and when she heard herself addressed thus, she paused, turned, and asked, "Do you know me then, that you address me thus by my name?"

"I know you only as the fairest singer ever seen, though indeed it is no surprise that one of your names is that of the skylark. Be assured, though, that I am not to be feared, though I may look a wild and lawless man, having not lived within walls these many weeks."

Now Lethanerri was not careless, having lived all her days on the Border between the Land of the Elder Folk and the Wild Lands, but when she looked carefully on this tall dark stranger with the grim face, she knew with the knowing of her people that he meant no harm for her, at the least.

It is time now to look to happenings further away, in a land less amenable to freedom of action for anyone, in Vandethair of the Warlock Lord.

Ghuadikh the Goblin-chief stood in the presence of the Warlock Lord himself. It was not the first time, nor would it be the last, but as always, he was uncomfortable about it. The Warlock Lord's voice spoke from a hood hiding the face which Ghuadikh had no desire to see. For the Warlock Lord could just as easily order his painful death as his glorification, and would do either if it suited any purpose of his, including such a small one as simply terrorizing any rebellion out of the rest of the biarighs.

"You will go far South, to the land of Cymruthair, and take away the Crystal Crown from the king of that land."

Ghuadikh knew what was expected of him, and it galled him. "My master has, then, a plan for placing us in such a position unseen. Will the Great one deign to inform this his slave as to his insignificant part in the plan?"

"Beware," said the voice, "You sound too human, too much like the other crawlers and traitors and night-spawn of the caverns that creep about seeking favours and hate within them. I know biarighs better than that, and I know that you hate the part you play; therefore play it not too well, lest I suspect you of the vices I know in the hearts of the others I spoke of."

"My master knows and sees all, and knows what my heart says."

"One of two things will happen to you: You will cease to be my most efficient captain, or you will make too great a slip on that borderline of efficiency and insolence; when either happens, I will have a new Captain. I have thirty werewolves to bear you and your folk out onto the plain ere morning, and on the day that you reach the Golden Trees, you will communicate with me, and by my arts I will hide you so that unless you stand openly in full sight for a greater length of time than is likely, you will remain unseen. Though the power of Guillen Termythnan is no inconsiderable thing, I will keep the shelter over you for a week's time. During that time you will be able to ambush him, slay him, and take away the Crown. Do you understand?"

"All save the matter of communication. How is that to be done?"

The Warlock Lord gave him instructions and all else necessary, and dismissed him. He stepped out of the Audience room to find his troop awaiting him. Twenty-nine fine strong goblins, brute-faced, long-armed, stoop-shouldered dark-complexioned, hardy. Ten who bore short recurved bolts and dark-fletched arrows, twenty including himself who bore spear, shield and broad stabbing-sword. They leaned toward him, and he spoke. "Raiding, my lads, a raid of all raids, which will get us great reward from *Him*. A raid into the Whitehair's land, to smite their king and take the Crystal Crown. But look, lads, *He* does not send us to death; *He's* making an enchantment so they can't see us. And we ride the first part of the way, ride on shape-changers that go faster than wind, with the speed of things unnatural. So take up your packs, and let us be going."

They went out of the palace, down the broad stair, and mounted the waiting were-wolves. With a trumpet blast, they were away, dashing down the ways of the city, shouting, hallooing, sounding wild horns, and clashing shields and spears. Out of the city, down the broad roadways, through the night's passing, laughing and shouting their rude jests as they flew down the dark stone road that lay broad before them in the weak moonlight that came through the clouds. Up, up, went the hurtling cavalcade, through the great pass of the mountains, then down again, through the land of Arkad that did not yet fully acknowledge the rule of their master. Arkads shuddered and shivered in their beds as the sounds arose in the morning, and made signs to keep the evil away, and only breathed properly again when the sounds had died away again in the distance. At last, having been borne more than a day and a half's march along their way, the goblins were finally forced to dismount, just before the sun began to rise.

The were-beasts left, dashing off out of the sight of their erstwhile riders to change their shapes again. The goblins all collapsed on the ground, and some began to sleep.

Ghuadikh began to put them to work erecting tents. "Up you lazy sons of the mine-pits! If you're awake and working under the sun, you won't suffer so bad, but if you lie here with no shelter, and sleep in the sunlight, you'll be doing no marching for another full day. And you know what *He'll* say to dawdling. I've got a long memory, and I'll turn in anyone who slacks, if I don't deal with him myself. So move."

Marahki and Sholkadha, balked and grumbled, but Ghuadikh, with the expertise of years, asserted his authority with the butt of his spear, and marked them down in his mind to be watched.

Meantime, Lethanerri, though not putting forth her complete trust immediately, walked all of the morning in the wood with Ardan, talking of many and various things. He told her of his life in the Lands of the Eastern Waste, of battle against the Nangs, and of customs of the desert. She in turn told him of herself. How her mother, as a girl, had been stolen by the Nangs, taken from them by the Eniyan Ii Igbo (the people of the jungle) of Kormotr, sold by them to a Tyuridan innkeeper, and rescued from there when the *Zakkur-Biarighs*, the flying goblins, and descended and destroyed the town of Cerach, seeking Lhoran the Tall who was on his way to destroy the dark hold in the Hills of Darkness. Lhoran brought her home, and wed her, and there they lived on the Edge of Cymruthair. She told of her brothers, grim Chorrin the Warrior, and smiling Huirrin the singer, and showed him many fair things to be found in Cymruthair.

As the day wore on, she trusted him more, and brought him at last to her parents. Lhoran, by the standards of the Elder Folk, was yet young, but he had great wisdom, and was accounted as one of respectability. He was a noble old person, and when first Ardan saw him, he was armed and armoured in chain-mail made by himself, with his long sword Bialyn at his side. His features were slim and rounded, his grey eyes serious, and a long green feather in his helm made him appear somewhat less unfeeling than the first view showed. Only a little behind him came Shirella, his wife, and mother to Lethanerri, fair and shining in a long green gown with a belt of golden leaves about her waist.

When they heard what she had to say of Ardan, and what he had to say of himself, they gravely invited him to remain there with them while they sought to find what the fate could be that awaited him. In part from desire for company, in part because of attraction to Lethanerri, and in part for the help they could give, he accepted. A messenger was sent off to Guillen Termythnan, since if someone was to find his fate in Cymruthair, it was best for Cymruthair to discover what that fate might be, lest it be detrimental to Cymruthair as well.

Now Ardan, being a courteous and careful man, was able to make himself fairly well-liked thereabouts, and he knew enough of the Elder Tongue that he could discuss things with them, and read their books of lore, from which he learned much. A feeling came to Lhoran that the fate of Ardan would concern powers which he did not fully understand, so the Elder one began to instruct him in the use of powers.

Ardan, for his part, learned well, and though he had not great skill in all such matters, nor great time to learn, he was able to learn well enough to do one or two of the most powerful enchantments. He was able to use the Third and Second Words, which would give him command of great Power for a time, though the Second Word would mean his death if he maintained its burden for long. He was shown the First Word, which Mortal Men may master after many years, and which Elder Folk use only rarely and with caution, but he did not even make the first steps toward attaining it.

Now these words, as he was cautioned, would give him power to match most of the present wizards, and some measure of protection against the rest. Any wizard likely to seek his harm would probably be at least a lesser servant of the Warlock Lord, and many of those would not be much deterred by either Word. Such a case would call for quickness of thinking and action.

One day, about fifteen days after the meeting of Ardan and Oruneal, Ghuadikh and his goblins reached the edge of Cymruthair. The time had come to communicate with his Master. He took a large silver bowl from his pack, traced with figures of horror, things not good to look upon, and runes unreadable that brought a shudder even to a hardened goblin.

This he gave to Marahki and Sholkadha to be filled with blood, a task they would enjoy somewhat, even though he assigned it in a way to make it seem a punishment. Then, he erected his tent so as to perform the proper magic in private. He had no fear of rebellion while he was not watching, for his troop would all be on their best behaviour while he was communicating with the Master of them all.

After he had followed his instructions, the rest did not take long at all. His Master said, after acknowledging the request for the promised protection, "I feel a strangeness here, of something that I have not sensed before. Strange things are fated to happen, and I do not comprehend them. Bring me a prisoner on your return, that I may attempt to discover more."

"As you command it, master," suddenly the goblin spoke again, "What is to happen after we ambush the Whitehair's King? I think that the most powerful enchantment will not save us forever from those who will search for us after that."

"At this moment, you are near to a circle of standing stones built long ago. Like many things built innocently by Men, it has been turned to my service, and when you are there, I will know. Be there for nightfall and a few hours thereafter, and I will bring you out. Now go on, and do not forget my prisoner."

And so the goblins went down, and for the first time, goblin feet trod under the Golden Trees, and their feet made marks in the grass of the Forbidden Lands. But so strong was the enchantment of the Warlock Lord that those who saw the footprints were misled as to their origin, and none sought to look too deeply into the matter.

Now Guillen Termythnan was ancient, and had been one of those who had fought the battles in Elffanthum, far Elderhome that was lost when the Pact of Evil was accomplished, and the Lords of Darkness loosed on Mortal Men. Ancient he was, and venerable, long of beard and thought, as the saying of his people went, and on a day some thought persuaded him to don the Crystal Crown, and see what might be seen.

As was his custom, he surveyed the Elder Land first. Away to the West all was calm. South toward the sea (Ah the Sea, the Sea, and the sun's scarlet setting on lost Elffanthum!) there was no danger. Nor was anything to be feared from the East and the Eastern Waste. And to the North-- to the North he could see nothing. But then he could see again. There was no anger, but there was a hint of some malevolent force.

With all the Power at his disposal, he could see that there was a danger to the North, but that it was so covered that he could see nothing of it. Indeed, the only way he could recognize it was by the barrier hiding it. He sent out the word for all the people to be watchful, for it was certain that a danger was abroad. However, there was no question of setting everyone to watch the North, lest the presence of the barrier be but a trick to hide another attack from elsewhere.

Long he strove at the matter of the barrier, and recognized at last that by a long process he could indeed break it down, but by that time, the attack or whatever approached would be over, since he recognized it for a stratagem of the Warlock Lord, who knew his own power well. At last he lay aside his Crystal Crown, and spoke to Thruathan Cynireal Greymantle who would be King after him, saying, "Long have I sought for the answer of this riddle, and many days have I striven with this evil matter. Let us go out, let us ride, for I would feel clean wind and clean rain on my face again."

So out they rode, but they had not gone far from the King's hall when Ghuadikh's band rose out of ambush, and attacked them. The King was slain almost immediately, but Thruathan had drawn his sword and defended himself, even when his horse died under him, all the time sounding an alarm on his small horn. With his back against a tree, he killed five of them before a band of armed Elves rode out of the city they had just left. The goblins, seeing this, fled, but they took the Crystal Crown along. They bore Guillen back in sorrow to his town, singing this lament:

*"Limith, limith, brha ghal limith nha y an du fetoa,*
*Lanissim, lanissim, lanissim!*
*Ychaelotu rythn ghal fecatha;*
*Femher ychamu y lhimitoth ghal;*
*Lenellotu ennita brha andonume feminnima!"*

*"Sorrow, sorrow, great our sorrow for the one who has fallen,*
*Grieve, grieve, grieve!*
*Autumn to our hearts has come;*
*The shining in our darkness is put out;*
*The wings of the wind have taken great wisdom!"*

Thruathan Greymantle did not spend great time in mourning, but set out immediately to hunt down those who had stolen the Crystal Crown. He knew well that, it would be invaluable for the Warlock Lord, and nigh disastrous for the rest of the world. It was a strange thing, though, that the goblin trail was almost impossible to follow. At times, it would be visible, but then would become faint, disappear, or lead off in another direction and disappear, leaving the trackers adrift with no sign of the trail.

It chanced that Lethanerri had gone a-wandering, by a secret spring where she was to meet Ardan later. A feeling came to her that all was not well, and as she looked around in preparation to flee, she saw brutish faces leering up at her from the bushes. This time, obviously, there was harm in store, and she lept up to flee. A whip lashed out, catching her ankle and bringing her down, and before she could do anything else, her hands were bound before her and she was led off at a run in the midst of a goblin troop.

Ghuadikh the Goblin-captain was pleased with himself. He had taken that cursed crown with a loss of but five , one of whom had been the troublemaker Sholkadha. They had taken a prisoner, a Whitehair woman, who would provide good amusement when they were home; as a reward, *He* might allow them to help in the gathering of information.

When Ardan came to meet Lethanerri, he wore no armour but his helm, and a sword at his side, using a spear as a walking, staff. It was the custom for those who lived in the borders of Cymruthair to go armed at all times, and he saw no reason to be different. He had spent the morning in study with Lhoran, who though a good teacher, was inclined to demand the utmost from his pupils. Ardan's mind was presently awhirl with new things he had just learned, and the walk was good. He came to the meeting-place, and did not see the Elf-maiden.

He was not at once concerned, for he thought she was only walking nearby. However, walking beside the stream, he found the soft ground where she had fallen, and the mud trampled by many feet. Fear came to him first, and as he read the signs, it turned to rage. As he looked away in the direction of the track, it seemed to glow faint, waver, disappear. He started out in that direction anyhow.

By this time, the limit was coming to the barrier of the Warlock Lord. It was not that he could no longer hold the barrier through lack of strength, but that the rest of his domains must be cared for. Already, a band of goblins were chafing under his rule, teetering on the edge of making themselves autonomous. As well, some of his emissaries to the tribes of the Wild Lands were being menaced, some already dead. Thus the goblins must look out for themselves; pursuit by this time would be so confused that they would have a good start.

Thus it was that only a little after he had begun, Ardan found the trail of the goblins wide and plain. He was nearing the edge of the wood when the messenger arrived at Lhoran's home to tell him of Guillen's death, and warn him of the Goblins' approach. They would not miss Lethanerri until later in the evening, and when they did discover her abduction, it would be morning before a prepared expedition could set out. Ardan moved swiftly along the trail, at a quick trot that would still allow him not to miss anything such as a splitting up of the group. By late afternoon, he was out of the wood, and could see a knot of figures toiling up the slope of a hill far away. He set out running. Nigh an hour later, he checked himself, as by instinct, for something seemed wrong ahead. A moment later, a goblin rose out of the tall grass drawing a bow.

Turning the spear in his hand, Ardan threw it, then ran forward, bending low. The arrow went wider than he expected, then saw the archer falling backward with the spear in his chest, while another, spear ready, came up out of the grass as well. Ardan's sword came out, and though an armoured man with a spear has the advantage over the swordsman, he used a trick and downed the goblin. It came to him that the bow would be useful, so loth as he was to take what a goblin owned, he went from there with the bow and arrows, following the clear track.

It was twilight when he came in sight of the great stone-circle, and his suspicions were confirmed when he saw a quick movement. They were up there, and probably all of them, encamped in a perfect defensive position. An attack on them would be nearly impossible. He was not planning an attack however, but a matter of creeping up on them, and taking the maid out by stealth.

He began to stalk then, crawling by inches through the grass. When night fell, he could move faster, but until then he must hide his movement.

Far to the North, however, in a deep cavern, there hung a group of beasts with somewhat birdlike heads, but jaws full of teeth, and leathery wings. Suddenly, a strange crystal lit up the cavern with a bluish light, and a coaxing voice began to speak, "Awake, awake, my pretties, up and away, spread great wings, fly, fly, swift as all the winds, away and away, southward to a small task, only a small one, then home, and a good reward. Up, now, strong wings in dark sky, away, fly away, with the night before us."

Harsh cries, fearsome cries, a rush for the cave's mouth, and one by one they launched themselves forth into the sky. High they went, but the people felt t their passing, and shivered.

Ardan was quite near the standing stones, When something passed over that caused him to shiver; he heard a harsh cry from the sky, then suddenly there were a number of flying creatures coming down in the midst of the stones. Immediately, he realized what was happening, and rose to his feet, readying his bow.

The light was too dim, he realized, and began to run forward, but the goblins had been prepared. All had been ready to mount, and before he had covered half of the remaining seventy-five yards, they were aboard and flying, laughing mockingly. He loosed an arrow, but missed, then began to run after them. His face to the sky, he ran like a wild man, cursing. His mind tried to tell him that he only imagined he could hear the harsh cries, out his heart would not listen, until he caught his foot in a tangle of grass and fell, knocking out his breath.

For some time, he lay weeping on the ground, weeping with the frustration and rage at his failure. Finally, he took hold of himself. "As father said, 'He who cannot keep his head may lose it– at the neck.' I have been the greatest of fools this day. Had I returned to Lhoran immediately, we should have set out on an expedition ahorse, and they should not have escaped us.

"Well, I have no  choice but to go on; to return now would be too much delay, but I cannot follow until morning."

After careful consideration, he made plans. He was about a day and a half's journey (but he could make it less) from the Jungle of Kormotr, and the beasts had been flying in exactly that direction. Therefore, they were gone to the Hills of Darkness; but the goblins would probably be going on to the land of Vandethair. Now, the Jungle was definitely not his country; therefore, he would be safer to skirt it. He had seen Cymrutha maps of all Known country in that direction, and as an expert campaigner had managed to memorize most of the land ahead.

Between the Jungle and the Hills was the territory of Tyurid. That was a chancy land, some of the folk in it being friendly, others not, so he had best not go too deeply into that either. After passing the Jungle, he would begin to swing slightly East, so that he would cut the biarigh's trail somewhere as they began to move to the Northwest to their home.

He managed to kill a rabbit the next morning, and made a water-bag from the skin, roasting the flesh. Some he ate, some he took along with him. He moved himself at a paced trot, working out the stiffness from yesterday's exertion and the night's fitful sleep. Gradually he increased his pace, endeavouring to set a speed that would not hear him out, but would enable him to make his speed increase with the days to come.

The Goblins would have about five days start on him, but he knew that they would also know that, and that would induce them to slack off, and he could increase his speed and very likely overtake them before they reached home.

Later that morning, by chance he met an Asbalnian Outrider, a rider of the Wild Lands, who sold him a blanket and a sturdy pair of shoes at a very cheap price. On he went, running for a time, then walking, then running again.

By the end of the third day, he had passed by the Jungle, and was moving slightly to the East. Early morning of the fifth day found him on the Great Caravan Road that leads from the Hotlands to Tyurid, and he guested that night with a caravan on their way home, to Merribo of Shurim in the Hotlands.

In the afternoon of the sixth day, he saw a small band of Dumnovai, small naked men with oblong shields and short spears, but they either did not see him, or ignored him. He also saw, a little later, a band of Harvatai in their war-wagons, but their minds were set on a greater prize somewhere, and They did nothing more than shout insults at him.

Things had not gone so well for Ghuadikh the Captain. They had been landed in the midst of the Hills of Darkness, and it had taken them until midmorning to follow the tortuous path out. By then his troop were on the verge of mutiny, and he had had to allow them to rest. When he finally got them moving again, he discovered that no matter how cruelly he beat her, Lethanerri could not keep up their pace. The fact of the slowed pace gave his troop more incentive to become slack, as though they needed it.

Ardan, having crossed their trail on the morning of the sixth day, was not only three days behind them. He would have caught them sooner, but he had to hunt for food, while they carried most of theirs. His time with Lhoran had not been wasted, and he was able, by knowledge of the means of speaking with them, to send messages to Lhoran by songbirds.

On the morning of the eleventh day, he found that he had spent the previous night only a matter of five miles from them, so he kept on the trail waiting for the night. While they were better able than he to see at night, they would also be less alert, with some of them resting.

Carefully and quietly, he came up on them. Lethanerri, worn and weary though she was, was being forced to work as a slave for them all. They had reached the top of a mountain pass, and in morning would be safe from the sun under their Master's perpetual gloom that ruled the skies there. By evening, they would be celebrating their reward within the city of their Master.

Ardan marked the position of the sentries, and readied his bow. If he could reach a certain point, he could probably kill at least two of the three before it was noticed. After that, he would shoot as many of the others as possible, lead them off on a chase out of the camp, circle back, and take Lethanerri.

His first arrow was accurate, and the goblin made no sound, simply slumped at his post. As he took up his next arrow, he saw something happening in the camp. Lethanerri, too weary to stand, had seated herself on the ground, and one of the troop demanded she bring him something. Because she was slow in complying, he struck her with a whip.

All this Ardan saw out of the corner of his eye as he drew the bow; he loosed swiftly, saw the goblin fall, then turned his next arrow to the one with the whip. Fair and true was his shot, and that one fell back as well. He had thrust a handful of arrows into the ground before him, and he began at once to shoot fast. He killed one other before the first shout was heard, then aimed at the chief.

The chief, however, leaped up, grabbed his packsack, and vanished into the darkness. Arden's arrow pierced his arm. The goblin-band had originally had ten archers, but two of these died fighting Thruathan, and another when he had ambushed Ardan. A fourth had been one of the sentries, and a fifth had been the one with the whip. Ardan, knowing the danger was greatest from the archers, shot another, but by now all were alerted, and running for safety. He shot another spear-bearer just before that one reached a large rock, and then they were gone. A harsh order sounded out from beyond the light of their fire, and two arrows hissed past his head. A group of spearmen rushed out, and he shot another before he saw that several of them were going for the Elf-maiden.

Remembering the things he had been told about the powers of the Words, he stood and spoke the Third Word. He saw, vaguely, that his whole body had began to shine, and his spear was a bar of light. The goblins halted, then scattered. He bounded down the slope, and those dragging Lethanerri away stopped to fight, then changed their minds and ran. One did not ran fast enough, and Ardan struck him down, then grasped Lethanerri by the hand and led her away to a place he had previously chosen.

The goblins, however, did not choose to come after them, but fled along the road. Lethanerri said, "No words will suffice for what I would say, only let it be known that I am grateful."

"I am but sorry I could not come sooner."

"One thing remains; they have still the Crystal Crown. If The Warlock Lord obtains that, all the world is in danger."

"But who has it? They will have scattered."

"Their chief, he who first fled. He has it in his pack."

"So that is why he would not abandon it. But I would not leave you defenceless."

"I will come along. I would not attempt to retrace my steps alone without dire need, nor would I wish to send you alone into further peril after what you have braved on my account."

"I would not go either, were the anger not so great."

They set out, then, but found it nigh impossible to keep to the path. At the last, They stopped to rest, sleeping in turns until the dawn. Dawn was late there, by reason of the very gloom of the skies above the Warlock Lord's dominion.

In the meantime, Ghuadikh, Marahki, and four others were fleeing ahead. After a time, they slowed to a walk, still remaining wary. Ghuadikh could hear Marahki talking to two of the others behind him. "Look", whispered the Captain, "That *khratsob* Marahki is making plots to take the glory and praise away from the ones who've earned it. Stick by me, and I'll see you get a promotion."

Behind them, an arrow slid out of a quiver; Ghuadikh turned and threw his spear, transfixing the archer, whose arrow struck the other goblin beside Ghuadikh. Ghuadikh leaped forward and parried Marahki's first blow, and cut him down, while the goblin to whom he had made the promise attacked the remaining one. In a moment, only the two of then remained.

"Well done," declared the chief. "I'll put you on the good side of my report; should go on the next list for promotions. You're Orikhrad, aren't you?"

"That's right, sir. Never did like that Marahki; he was up from the mine-pits, and tried to make everybody forget it."

Though they tried, Ardan and Lethanerri could not catch up with the goblins, partly because they met up with a party of five of the survivors who insisted on fighting. Ardan used his bow, but it came to sword-strokes, and lasted a little longer than they would have wished. In any case, they, were close enough to recognize the goblin-chief as he went in the gates of the city.

They sat there for a moment, knowing that their attempt was useless, and Ardan was about to suggest they begin to go back when an old grey man appeared around the edge of one of the great ash-pits that stood be side a mine-shaft. "If you seek a way into the city, I know of one such."

"Much good would it do us; in the Warlock Lord's domain, what might such as we do?"

"By going unexpectedly, you might accomplish much. I leave it to you, but there is a way; you will find that at the foot of one of the towers, a clump of brush grows. Behind that is a place, hitherto unnoticed, where the wall is beginning to crumble. One could go through there, and find oneself on the street that leads to the palace kitchen. Once within, directions are clearly marked to the throne-room where the Lord will receive the goblin."

When he had finished speaking, the old man walked back beyond the ash-pile, and when Ardan rushed forward to find him, he had disappeared in the rough ground. After a little discussion, they made their decision. The Warlock Lord would be so much taken up with having the Crystal Crown in his possession that they might come close enough to reclaim it. After that, by virtue of its own power, it should protect them from enchantments long enough to effect some sort of escape. As a last resort, they might attempt to destroy it.

They went seeking, and found all as they had been told. Indeed, the wall was in such bad condition that most of it was already gone, and it took little effort to get through. Following the old man's directions, they found the door of the Palace kitchen. The guards there believed Ardan to be one of them until he struck one of them down with his spear, and the other was unable to do much more than stop the first stroke before he went down as well.

They went inside, and none of the slaves tried to stop them. Quickly, they found the antechamber where they waited with the others who had audiences with the Lord. The great door of the Audience Hall was just closing behind Ghuadikh, who had had his wound dressed before coming. They rushed forward, and thrust open the door, so that the surprised guards had no time to stop them. The Warlock Lord, robed and hooded, sat on a raised dais of grey stone, but he was not taken quite so much by surprise. "Guards!" he called, "Take these away."

Ardan handed his sword to Lethanerri, then spoke the Second Word. Goblins surrounded them, but were afraid to attack him. The Warlock Lord spoke again, "I hope you do not think I am unfamiliar with that word. It will but make you somewhat more difficult to vanquish, but you shall die in my dungeon. The power of that word cannot harm me."

"Ah,"said Ardan, "But what if I merely do this?"

And he smote the dais before him, as the Warlock Lord reached up to unhood himself. The stone of the dais cracked and splintered, a great crack running up to go under the Iron Throne, which toppled and fell, itself shattering, and throwing the Warlock Lord to earth.

While he was stunned and unconscious, Ardan stepped forward, picked up the crown, and laughed. At that moment, Ghuadikh threw a spear, which wounded Ardan badly, so that he almost fell. But the guards and goblins, disheartened by their leader's fall, fled, and Ardan and Oruneal also went out. Ardan, however, soon grew so faint that he must lean on the Elf-maiden for support. Thus they escaped the town, for rumours were flying around about what had happened, and some looked for attackers outside, some sought assassins or rebels inside, and others simply fled the city. A little outside the city, however, they could no longer go on, for Ardan was fainting for loss of blood, though Lethanerri had sought to bind up the wound, the spear that had caused it had had some foul enchantment on it.

In the moment when she was most despairing, she looked up and saw a band of riders approaching. As they neared, her heart leaped, for her father led them, and her two brothers were with him, as well as many others whom she knew from the land of the Golden Trees. To save that They fought a way out of that land would be simple; however, compared to the deeds already done, it does seem so. The arts of the Elder folk eventually proved equal to the enchantment of Ardan's wound, so that he lived, and was wed to Lethanerri with much joy on all sides deep within the Wood of the Stars.

So was the foremost of the Half-elder houses founded, by the marriage of the maiden named Lethanerri to Ardan the Grim. Nor is the tale ended here, for some of that family had a great part in the final fall and death of the Warlock Lord of Vandethair. But that story is written in another book, and is longer than may be told here.

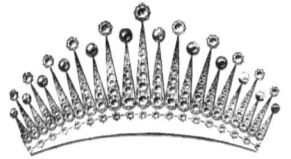

# About the Author

J. P. Wagner was both a sci-fi/fantasy writer and a journalist. While his editorials and informative articles could be found in publications such as the Western Producer and the Saskatoon Star Phoenix, Railroad Rising: The Black Powder Rebellion is his first published novel.

A self-proclaimed curmudgeon, but known to his family as a merry jokester, his words have brightened many lives. Sadly, J. P. Wagner passed away in 2015 before the publication of Railroad Rising: The Black Powder Rebellion.

While this may be the last book he finished before he died, it doesn't mean that this was his only book. In addition to his career in journalism, he wrote many novels throughout his lifetime. All of these works have been passed down to me, his daughter and now I will share them with you.

Read more at www.revjpwagner.com.